Trouble in the Black Hills

Penn Mullin

High Noon Books
Novato, California

Cover Design and Interior Illustrations: Damon Rarey

International Standard Book Number: 0-87879-962-1

7 6 5 4 3 2 1 0 9 8
3 2 1 0 9 8 7 6 5 4

You'll enjoy all the High Noon Books. Write for a free full list of titles, including:

Postcards from Europe - Set #976-1

Postcards from South America - Set #014-6

Contents

1 Ghost Village Ranch 1

2 The Sacred Pipe 9

3 Off to Mount Rushmore 16

4 The Four Presidents 21

5 A Man with a Phone 33

6 A Race to the Ranch 37

7 The Legend of the Sacred Pipe 41

All aboard! Juan; Mike, their van driver; Justin; Miss Lake, their teacher; Amy; and Lisa smile for the camera before taking off on their trip.

When Miss Lake's seventh grade class entered the President's *See America the Beautiful* contest, they didn't think they had a chance to win. It was fun thinking they might, so everyone wrote and sent in a short essay on "What Do You Like Best About Being an American?"

They could hardly believe it when the letter came. It said: "The essays sent in by four members of your class were outstanding. These students have won a three-week trip across the United States with their teacher. All expenses will be paid."

The class clapped when Miss Lake finished reading the letter and Lisa, Amy, Justin, and Juan went home to pack their bags.

CHAPTER 1

Ghost Village Ranch

"Ghost Village Ranch. I really like that name," Justin said. He read the sign over the log gate. "I can't wait to hear how it got that name!"

"John Rising Hawk will tell you. He has owned the ranch for many years," Mike the van driver said. "His great grandfather's village once stood here where the ranch is."

"I'm sure glad we're here," Amy said. "That was a long ride." She yawned.

"But it was pretty driving through the

Black Hills," said Miss Lake, their teacher.

"Why do they call them the Black Hills?" Lisa wanted to know.

"Remember all the dark green pine trees that covered the hills? That's where this part of South Dakota got its name," Miss Lake told her.

"OK, we're here!" Mike called out. He stopped the van beside a log building under the trees.

"Is this the ranch house?" Juan asked.

"Yes," Mike said. "And here comes John to greet us."

They saw a tall, thin Native American man coming towards the bus. He had a broad smile across his tanned face.

"Welcome, all of you," John said. "I'm glad you're here safely. Mike is a good driver, I know!"

"John, it's good to see you again!" Mike said. They shook hands. "It's been many years since I was here with you."

"Not much has changed," John said. "And that's good. Come on, everybody. I'll show you the bunkhouse."

They all followed John towards another long low building. There were two large rooms with bunks against the walls.

"This was where all the cowboys slept," John said. "That was back when we had a big herd of cattle here."

"So this is not a cattle ranch any more?" Miss Lake asked.

"No," John said. "I just keep busy with groups like yours who come to see Mount Rushmore."

"How far are we from Mount Rushmore?" Juan asked.

"Only a couple of miles," John said. "When they were carving the faces on the mountain, some of the workers stayed here."

"I can't wait to see it," Lisa said. "I can't believe the faces could be so totally huge!"

"And they look so alive, too!" John said. "You'll be amazed."

"So you're pretty busy running this place, John," Mike said.

"I sure am. And you remember my collection? It takes up a lot of my time, too." John smiled at him.

"What collection?" Justin asked.

"I have many things that belonged to my great grandfather, Hunting Bear. He was a Sioux chief in the 1870's. His village used to stand right here," John said. "It filled this whole meadow."

"What happened to it?" Amy asked.

"No one knows for sure," John answered. "One day it was here. A large village of fifty tepees. The next day it was gone. There was no sign of a battle. They just went away. But no one knows where."

"Is that why they call it the Ghost Village?" Lisa asked.

"Yes, that's right," John answered slowly.

"But you still have some things from the village?" Miss Lake asked.

"Yes, a few things were left behind," John said. "The people must have been in a great hurry. They left the most valuable treasure of all—the peace pipe of their tribe."

"And you still have this peace pipe?" Miss Lake asked.

"Yes, it is the most valuable thing I own." John lowered his voice. "I do not talk about it

Indian Women at Their Tasks

very much. There is danger that the wrong people will find out that the pipe is here. Then there would be bad trouble at Ghost Village Ranch."

CHAPTER 2

The Sacred Pipe

"Now will you show us the Sacred Pipe?" Justin asked John after dinner.

"Yes, I'll go get it. Wait just a minute," John told the group. He went off into another room. Soon he was back. He carried something that was wrapped in a brown cloth.

"I want you to promise me something." John spoke very softly. "You must promise not to share the secret that the Sacred Pipe is here. Do you all agree?" he asked.

"Yes," everyone answered quickly.

John unwrapped the pipe slowly. "This is buffalo calf skin around it. You can tell it is very old. It is so thin now." Inside the skin was a dark red wooden pipe about 18 inches long. A small round hollow bowl sat on top of it near the end.

"It's beautiful!" said Miss Lake. "I can tell that it took a lot of work to make."

"Is that a fan hanging from the end of it?" Lisa asked.

"Yes, it is made of eagle feathers," John said.

"Just think how old those are," said Mike. "That eagle lived around here more than one hundred years ago."

Everyone got a chance to hold the pipe.

"Was smoking the pipe part of a ceremony?" Miss Lake asked John.

"Yes," he said. "The leaders of the village smoked it when they wanted to make a prayer for help. And they smoked it to offer prayers of thanks, too. The pipe was used at many important times in village life."

"I guess they guarded their pipe very carefully, didn't they?" Juan asked.

"Yes, they did. If something happened to its sacred pipe, a village felt lost," said John. "So the pipe was always well cared for."

"Are there many pipes like this still

around?" Lisa asked.

"No," John answered. "This is one of just a few left from a Sioux tribe. So it has to be well guarded."

"Has anybody ever tried to steal it?" Amy asked.

"Well, someone broke into the ranch house this spring. I think they were looking for the pipe. I'm glad I had hidden it well," John said.

"How did they know the pipe was here?" Mike asked.

"I don't know. Only my special friends know about the pipe," John said. "But secrets get told. And people will pay big money for a pipe like this."

"You mean someone would steal it and then sell it?" Justin asked.

"Yes. I'm afraid so," John said.

"Hey, gang, we've got a big day tomorrow," Miss Lake told the kids. "We're off to Mount Rushmore! Maybe we should head out to the bunkhouse."

Justin groaned. "But I want to hear more about the pipe. It's still early."

John Rising Hawk laughed. "The pipe will still be here tomorrow. We'll look at it again then. I'm glad you're interested. Now, off to the bunkhouse!"

Everybody stood up to leave. John got

ready to wrap up the pipe. Suddenly a man stepped out of the shadows and into the light.

"Excuse me, John. I'm having trouble with the lights out in the barn," he said. "I was working on the truck. Could you come out and give me a hand?"

"Well, OK, Steve. I guess I could. I didn't hear you come in the door. Have you been standing there long?" John asked the tall, heavy Native American man.

"No, not long. I just let myself in. I saw you were busy," Steve said. He looked at the pipe lying on the table.

"Well, I'll be out in a few minutes, Steve. You go on ahead," John told him.

Steve went out into the darkness.

John quickly wrapped up the pipe. His face looked worried.

"Who is he, John?" Mike asked.

"Steve's new on the ranch. I just hired him last month," John said. "He's good with engines and I've got some old trucks that need work. I should have had you all meet him. But he surprised me so much. I didn't know he was in the room until he said something."

"You look upset," Mike told John.

"I guess I am. I don't like being surprised like that. Or watched when I don't know it," John added. "Especially when the Sacred Pipe is lying out on the table."

CHAPTER 3

Off to Mount Rushmore!

"Blueberry pancakes! I think I'm going to like ranch life!" Justin sat down at the long table piled high with breakfast food.

"Is there any food in the world you don't like?" Amy laughed.

"I haven't met one yet," Justin answered. He began helping himself to the pancakes.

"I'm happy to see this hungry bunch!" laughed Al, the ranch cook. He came out of the kitchen and walked around the table.

"I love these muffins, Al," Miss Lake said. "You're going to make us all fat."

"You won't get fat up here. John will hike you too far for that. Just wait until tonight. You'll be hungry all over again. There's lots of long trails up at Mount Rushmore," Al said. His smile lit up his round face. Like John, he was also Native American.

Just then John came into the dining room. "What kind of stories is Al telling you?" he laughed. "The trails aren't too steep. You'll see. But be sure to wear comfortable shoes. And bring a jacket. It can get windy."

"The van is ready to go," Mike said.

"We'll leave right after breakfast then. I'll

tell the kids some of Mount Rushmore's history as we drive up there," John said.

"Sounds like a good idea. We didn't tell them much before we got here. I knew you could do a better job of it," Mike told John.

"They're a great bunch of kids. I like how they are interested in everything," John said.

"Is it OK to go get in the van?" Amy asked Mike.

"Sure. We'll be right out," he answered.

"One more sip of coffee," Miss Lake said. "Then I'm ready.

Finally everyone was in the van. Mike drove slowly towards the front gate.

"We've got a beautiful day to see Mount

Rushmore," John told the kids. He was sitting at the front of the bus. "Who can tell me the four presidents whose faces are carved up on the mountain?"

Lisa raised her hand. "Lincoln, Jefferson, Washington, and Roosevelt."

"Great! You get an A for the day, Lisa. OK, I want to tell you about the famous sculptor who carved the faces," John said. "His name was Gutzon Borglum. He wanted to carve a great national monument. So he came out to South Dakota in 1924 to look for the right mountain."

"Why did Borglum choose South Dakota?" Amy asked.

"The Black Hills have some of the world's oldest and hardest stone. It is called granite," John said. "Borglum knew that his monument would last a long time if he carved it out of South Dakota granite."

"Here's the front gate," Mike said. The van pulled out onto the main road. "Mount Rushmore, here we come!"

There was an old truck hidden in the trees near the front gate. Inside it a man watched as the van drove out of sight. Then the man quickly drove back towards the ranch house.

CHAPTER 4

The Four Presidents

The van rolled slowly up the long windy road. There were thick pine forests everywhere the kids looked.

"All this land once belonged to my people," John told them. "There was everything they needed here. Good hunting and fishing. Then gold was discovered in the Black Hills. The Sioux land became very valuable. The United States Government tried to buy the land from the Sioux."

Mount Rushmore—The Beginning

"Did they sell it?" Justin asked.

"No, they refused," John said. "So the government finally sent them to live on a reservation. It was a terrible time for our people."

"How did you get back your family's land?" Juan asked.

"My grandfather saved some money. He came and bought back the land," John said. "I am very glad he did. Look, we are coming to Mount Rushmore! In a minute you'll see the faces. Mike, there's a great view just ahead off the road."

Mike parked the van at a lookout point.

"Well, there they all are!" John said

proudly. "Washington, Jefferson, Lincoln, and Roosevelt."

Everyone looked up at the four giant faces carved into the mountainside.

"They're huge!" Lisa said.

"Washington's face is sixty feet tall," John said. "And guess how wide his eyes are!"

"Five feet?" Justin asked.

"Eleven feet!" John said. "And a mouth that is 18 feet wide."

"How could somebody get up there to carve the faces?" Juan asked. "They're so high."

"They had three different ways. Men worked in harnesses. These were straps that held their bodies tight against the mountain. They also had scaffolding. These were wooden platforms men stood on to do the carving. They were attached to the rock."

"Talk about scarey. One backwards step!" Amy rolled her eyes.

"That's one reason they built the moveable cages," John said. "They had wood sides that kept the workers from falling. The cages were moved on ropes. Then the workers could move all over the faces as they carved."

"Did anyone ever get killed up there?" Justin asked.

"No, they had a perfect safety record," John said. "Even with all that dynamiting."

"Dynamiting?" Juan asked.

"Yes, that's how they blasted away the outer layer of rock," John said. "Then they could get at the granite under it. That white granite is what they wanted to carve the faces in."

"Amazing no one was hurt," Mike said.

"That's for sure. Well, let's drive up to the main visitors' center. You can get a closer view from there," John said.

Soon they were all standing below the giant faces, looking up.

"What are all those rock piles under the faces?" Amy asked. "Was there a landslide?"

"No, those rocks were blasted off when the

faces were made," John said.

"Why did the sculptor choose this mountain?" Lisa asked.

"Well, Borglum needed a tall mountain. Then the faces could be seen for miles. Also, he needed a broad space of granite to carve in. And the mountain had to stand in sunlight," John said. "That way the faces could be seen almost all day."

"So I guess Mount Rushmore was the perfect place," Miss Lake said.

"Why is it called Mount Rushmore?" asked Justin.

"It was named for Charles Rushmore in the 1880's," John said. "He loved this mountain so much that people gave it his name."

"Kind of neat to have a mountain named after you," Amy said.

"Let's walk up this trail. It will take us closer to the mountain. And we can get away from all the people." John led the way up through the dark green pines.

They could look up at the white stone faces through the trees.

"It's so quiet," Lisa said. "All you can hear is the wind in the pines."

"There's something magical about this mountain," John said. "I can always feel it."

They came to a clearing in the trees.

"Let's stop here," John told the group. "Look what a clear view we have."

"Teddy Roosevelt's moustache looks so real," Miss Lake said. "Great details!"

"Why did these men get chosen to be on Mount Rushmore?" Juan asked.

"Well, the sculptor felt these were the four greatest men in American history. Washington because he founded our country and was the first president. Who can tell me about Jefferson?" John asked.

"Was he the one who wrote the Declaration of Independence?" Lisa asked.

"Yes. And when he was president he sent Lewis and Clark to explore the West. That was how this whole area became settled. Now who can say why Lincoln is up there?"

"He freed the slaves," Justin said.

"Yes, he helped Black people begin to have rights in this country," John added. "OK, Roosevelt is left. Who can tell about him?"

The kids didn't say anything. Miss Lake smiled and raised her hand.

"He built the Panama Canal when he was president," she said. "This canal cut through a thin strip of land between North and South America. Then boats could go this short way from the Atlantic to the Pacific Ocean."

"All famous Americans up there," John said. "A beautiful sight."

"How long did it take to carve it all?" Lisa asked John.

"Well, it was started in 1927. And it was finished in 1941," John said. "But sometimes work stopped. There wasn't enough money to pay the men. Borglum was always raising money for the project. The real working time was only six and a half years!"

Just then a man stepped into the clearing. He wore a green ranger's uniform.

"Hi. Are you folks heading back down to the Center?" he asked.

"Pretty soon," John answered. "We're still looking at the mountain."

"OK. Enjoy yourselves." The man waved

and went on down the trail.

John stared after him. "There was something strange about that man. I don't know what it is. But something doesn't feel right. He just didn't seem like a ranger to me."

The man disappeared from sight. Then he quickly took out a cordless phone from under his jacket. He carefully checked the trail behind him. Then he dialed a number.

CHAPTER 5

A Man with a Phone

"I want to get some souvenirs. Is it OK to go in the gift shop?" Lisa asked Miss Lake.

Now they were all back at the Visitors' Center again.

"Yes, Lisa. And, Juan, better get a postcard. It's your turn tonight to write one to our friends back at school," said Miss Lake.

Amy and Justin walked over towards the snack bar. Miss Lake, Mike, and John started back to the van.

"Hey, Justin, isn't that the ranger we saw on the trail?" Amy looked over towards a man standing in the trees. The man had his head bent down. He was talking into a cordless phone.

"Yes, I'm sure that's the same guy," Justin said. "He's the one John said didn't seem like a ranger."

"Let's walk over there by him. Maybe we can hear what he's saying," Amy said.

Then they walked towards the man with the phone. The man had his back to them. They started to walk past him on the path.

"OK, so you've still got 45 minutes," the man was saying into the phone. "They're just about to leave. Still in the gift shop and the snack bar. Keep looking. It's got to be there somewhere."

Amy and Justin kept on walking quickly down the path. They knew they didn't dare turn around. Did the man know they had heard him talking?

They kept on walking. The man was not following them. Finally they were far enough away. Now they could talk.

"Did you hear what he said? He's watching us. We've got to warn John!" Justin told Amy.

"He's talking to somebody back at the ranch. Somebody who's looking for the Sacred Pipe! Come on!" said Amy.

They ran through the trees. Branches whipped at their faces. Were they going towards the van? What if they got lost? They had to get back to John. They kept on running. Still no sign of the parking lot. Then they saw their red van through the trees. John was standing beside it.

"John, they're trying to steal the Sacred Pipe! We've got to get back to the ranch!"

CHAPTER 6

A Race to the Ranch

Mike drove as fast as he could on the mountain road. The ranch was now only fifteen minutes away.

"I just hope the police get there in time to stop the robbers. They said they would head right over when I called," John said. "You kids did good work. I'm sure glad you heard that phone call. But you took a chance getting close to that guy. I bet he could be mean."

"You were sure right about him, John.

You knew it as soon as you saw him on the trail," Amy said.

"He had stolen a ranger's uniform. I checked with the ranger station. He has already disappeared," John said.

"I bet he's taking a back road to your ranch," Mike said. He guided the van carefully around a curve.

"Probably right. I know it's Steve he's hooked up with. Steve got a good look at the Sacred Pipe last night. He waited till we were gone to start hunting for it," John said.

"This fake ranger probably followed us all day. He would call Steve on the phone. Then Steve knew just how much time he had left to

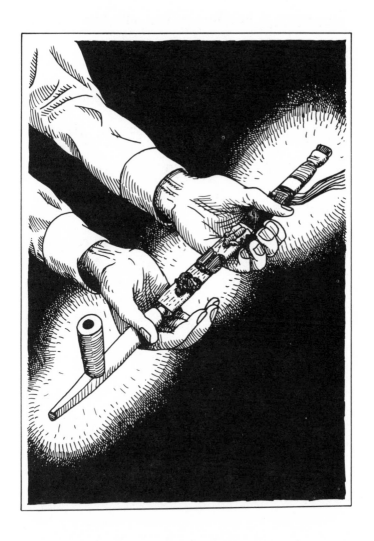

"Our words rise to you in this smoke."

find the pipe," Miss Lake said.

"He'll never find it." John smiled. "But I hate to think what he'll do to the ranch while he is looking. He will probably tear everything apart. I'm glad I hid most of my other special Sioux treasures, too."

"Here's the ranch now," Mike said. He drove through the front gate and started down the road. At the far end they could see the red flashing lights of a police car. It was parked by the ranch house. Had the robbers been caught? Was the Sacred Pipe safe?

CHAPTER 7

The Legend of the Sacred Pipe

They all jumped out of the bus at the ranch house. Two policemen ran up to meet them.

"They got away, John. They were just heading out of the gate when we got here. I don't know what stuff they took. But we sent two cars out after them," the policeman said. "I just hope we can catch them. They've been stealing Sioux treasures all over the West."

"Thanks, Pete," John said. "I've got to go check on the pipe." He ran into the house.

Mike followed him.

Soon John called out, "It's still here. It's safe! I knew it would be. But I just had to make sure." He came out into the hallway holding the Sacred Pipe in his hands. He was smiling.

Everyone gathered around John. They all wanted to touch the pipe. Just to make sure it was still there.

The rooms in the ranch house were a mess. Tables were turned over. Bookcases were knocked down. The robbers had been angry that they could not find the pipe.

Suddenly Pete rushed up to John. "They've got them! Their truck just had a flat tire. Those two guys won't be stealing any more. The truck was full of stuff they'd taken. Maybe some of it is yours."

"Great! I'm glad they're caught. I hate to think of their selling any Sioux treasures. There are so few left now," John said. "Amy and Justin, you helped catch those guys. I owe you a lot of thanks for what you did. You are great kids."

"I'm so glad they were caught," Amy said.

"Yeah, they derserved that flat tire. Bad luck, guys!" Justin laughed.

"Oh, I don't think bad luck had much to do with it," chuckled John.

"What do you mean?" Lisa asked.

"Well, there's a legend that goes with the Sacred Pipe of our tribe," John said softly. "Anyone who has ever tried to take it has had something bad happen to them."

"Really? Will you tell us about the other times and what happened to the people?" Lisa asked John.

John Rising Hawk smiled and sat down beside the fireplace. The kids sat down all around him. "Well, I remember one story that happened long ago," he began. "It was when the village stood in this meadow . . . "